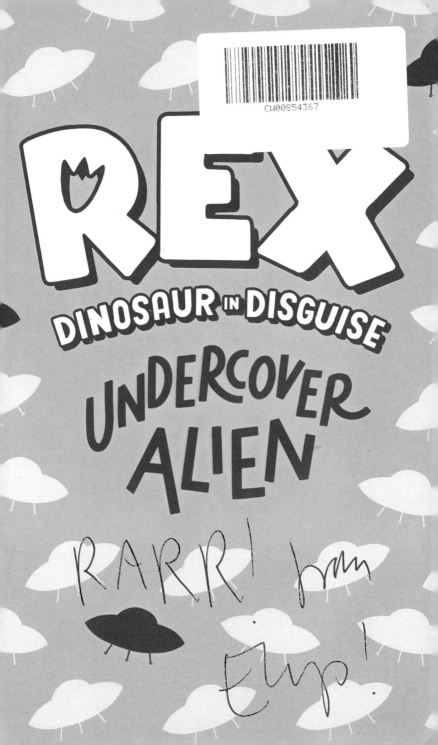

FOR BERTIE, WHO OCCASIONALLY SLEPT SO I COULD WRITE THIS BOOK

First published 2024 by Walker Books Ltd
87 Vauxhall Walk, London SE11 5HJ

2 4 6 8 10 9 7 5 3 1

© 2024 Elys Dolan

The right of Elys Dolan to be identified as author of
this work has been asserted in accordance with
the Copyright, Designs and Patents Act 1988

This book has been typeset in Stempel Schneidler,
Berliner Grotesk, Burbank Big Regular

Printed in China

British Library Cataloguing in Publication Data:
a catalogue record for this book is available
from the British Library

ISBN 978-1-4063-9771-0

www.walker.co.uk

WALKER
BOOKS

FSC
www.fsc.org
MIX
Paper | Supporting
responsible forestry
FSC® C144853

CHAPTER 1
MR FUZZELWUZZELWOOO

Rex's life was perfectly normal, just like any human's. He lived in a flat in the city with his roommate. He had a job as a PE teacher at the local school. He'd figured out how clothes work and thought wearing T-shirts and ties was "his thing". He could even make a lasagne with a crunchy Cheez Nubbins topping, which he was proud to say his roommate described as "acceptable". But the thing was, Rex wasn't a perfectly normal human; he was a dinosaur.

A dinosaur with a school fair to prepare for.

"I'm in charge of the endurance hopping competition for the grown-ups," said Rex, making the whole garden shake as he hopped on one foot.

Rex's best human friend, nine-year-old Sandra Shellman, put down the big pot of glue and said, "Fun! I'll come and watch."

As well as being a nine-year-old, Sandra was an expert investigator, specializing in mysteries. In fact, with the help of her friend Anish, she was the brains who first discovered Rex's secret identity. Now everyone at school knew that Rex was a dinosaur and mostly seemed OK about it. Rex stayed in disguise when he was out in the big wide world though. A dinosaur at the supermarket trying to buy shampoo attracts a lot of unwanted attention.

"Do you want to see the display for my stand?" Sandra spun round the huge piece of card she'd been working on.

"I love it," said Rex. "You used a lot of glue, didn't you?"

"You can never have enough glue," said Sandra. "I want someone to come with me to the sewers to hunt for the alligators!"

"What about Anish?"

"I think he's busy with the pet show. He and Bigfoot are getting Mr Fuzzelwuzzelwooo ready. Come on, let's give them a hand."

Sandra carefully pocketed her glue and Rex followed her over to the picnic table, where Anish and Rex's roommate, a yeti named Bigfoot, were fussing over something.

Rex crouched down and looked closely at the strange creature. It let out a grumpy little "weep!"

"What's this?" asked Rex.

"It's a guinea pig," said Sandra.

"Ninny pig?" said Rex. He still found some human words hard to say.

"Guinea pig," said Sandra.

"Grumpy pig?" said Rex.

"Guinea pig," said Sandra.

"Gwinty squid?" said Rex.

"Guinea… We'll work on this later." Sandra gave Rex a pat on the shoulder.

"I don't get it. What's it for?" asked Rex.

"It's a pet," said Sandra. She crouched down next to Mr Fuzzelwuzzelwooo and said:

Who's a cutey wooty little guinea piggy!

Rex wrinkled his nose. "It smells a little –" Rex looked for the word – "poopy."

Anish opened his eyes wide and said, "Mr Fuzzelwuzzelwooo has a delightful musk!"

There were lots of things about humans that surprised Rex, but he really didn't understand why Sandra and Anish, two of the most sensible humans he knew, turned into babbling jelly people when they talked about Mr Fuzzelwuzzelwooo.

"But it doesn't even talk," said Rex, more baffled than ever. "Isn't it boring? Even I talk."

"Boring?!" Outraged, Anish's mouth dropped open. "Mr Fuzzelwuzzelwooo is my friend!"

"Rex!" hissed Bigfoot. "You can't just tell people their pets are boring and smell like poop!" Bigfoot, even though he was a yeti, was more human than most humans.

Rex shuffled his feet. "But it does smell like poop. I'm just being honest."

"That's not the point," said Bigfoot.

Rex spread his little arms wide. "We didn't have pets in prehistoric times. If I'd gone around calling an Aquilops a 'cutey wooty whatsit', all the raptors would have laughed at me and then eaten the Aquilops."

"They might not have if the Aquilops was as cute as Mr Fuzzelwuzzelwooo here," said Sandra, giving the guinea pig a scratch. "Come on, we'd better go and set up at the fair. Nessy will be there already putting up the hook-a-duck stand and Dodo is bringing his burger van. And maybe you'll find a pet you do like at the pet show?"

"Maybe," said Rex, but he wasn't sure about that.

CHAPTER 2
THE FAIR

During the fair, several people had stopped at Sandra's stand to ask about the alligators. Ethan from 2F had even offered to come with her to find them and use his cat as bait.

Sandra peered into the crowd to look for her mum and dad and saw they were with her baby brothers, Larry, Gary and Barry, on the bouncy castle. Just then she caught sight of the very people she wanted to avoid.

Maddie used to be Sandra's best friend, but last term she had stopped talking to Sandra and started hanging out with two mean girls, both called Hannah. Sandra had better friends now, but the memory still made her stomach feel tight.

"Maddie! Look what the Shellman girl is up to!" said Hannah P, ignoring Sandra and pointing at her display.

"I'm right here," said Sandra. "You can talk to me."

"Shellman wants to go into the sewers?! And get covered in toilet scum!" said Hannah M.

"It's not that simple—" said Sandra.

Maddie turned to her. "I can't believe you're still hunting for mysteries. It's so babyish. Isn't one dangerous monster enough for you?"

Sandra knew when Maddie said "monster", she meant Rex. Maddie was not just very anti-mystery, she was very anti-dinosaur too. Last sports day, she'd discovered Rex was a dinosaur disguised as a PE teacher. She called the zoo to have him taken away and Rex escaped with Sandra's help. Rex says Maddie is the best wing-attack the netball team has ever had, so he doesn't mind giving her a second chance. Sandra hasn't forgiven her though.

"Rex isn't a monster; he's a dinosaur. And not just a dinosaur – he's also a PE teacher who right now is in charge of an endurance hopping competition— Oh, the competition!"

Maddie rolled her eyes as Sandra set off at a run. Sandra didn't care. She'd promised Rex she'd be there to watch.

She skidded to a halt next to Rex, who was watching closely for fouls.

"What did I miss?" said Sandra.

"Jade's mum got thirsty, Nadia and Ethan's stepdad sprained his ankle, so it's between Mr Dodo and Maddie's dad," said Rex, without taking his eyes off the hoppers.

"I didn't know Mr Dodo was so athletic," said Sandra.

"The prizes are being awarded by the mayor. Dodo is desperate to meet him. And I think Mr Beaumont is just very competitive," said Rex. He suddenly gave a blast of his whistle and shouted, "Foot on the floor! That's a foul, Mr Beaumont. Mr Dodo wins!"

"YESSSS!" Mr Dodo hopped triumphantly round the circle, taking in the applause from the crowd of parents and children.

Mr Beaumont turned to face Rex. "I did NOT put my foot on the floor. That cheating dinosaur just wants his friend to win!"

"That's not true!" said Rex. "I take fair hopping very seriously."

"Aye, we all saw your foot hit the ground, Beaumont!" Nessy yelled from her hook-a-duck stand. "Stop your whining and be a good loser."

That made Mr Beaumont angrier.

WEE SCUNNER!

"You can't believe her either!" he pointed at Nessy. "You can't trust any of these creatures. They go round disguised as humans when they're actually dangerous monsters!" Mr Beaumont scowled at Rex, flung his sweatband at him and stormed off.

"That didn't end how I wanted it to," said Rex.

"It was a fine competition, young Rex," said Dodo, patting him on the arm. "Come on, let's go and see Bigfoot and Anish at the pet show while we wait for the prize-giving. Mr Mayor, here I come!"

Sandra followed Rex and Dodo, thinking about how to tell Anish what had happened with Maddie and her dad. Once she was inside the tent, the sight took her mind off that problem entirely.

SNAKE

PARROT

RABBIT

DOG

STICK INSECT

CAT

"Have you ever seen so many guinea pigs in one place?" Anish shouted to Sandra from next to Mr Fuzzelwuzzelwooo. "I just know we'll win Best in Show."

"I don't know how the mayor will choose," said Rex. "I'm still not sure what's so great about goopy pigs."

A few guinea pig owners turned round to give Rex harsh looks.

Rex didn't notice though. "I suppose they're sort of the same shape as Cheez Nubbins, which is nice, but judging Cheez Nubbins would be easier. You could just put them in your mouth and see which one is tastiest."

The whole tent went quiet and stared at Rex.

CHAPTER 3
MR MAYOR

Rex sensed that he might have said something wrong.

"Does he … want to eat the guinea pigs like Cheez Nubbins?" said Mrs Horne, who worked in the school office.

"Did he call them goopy pigs?" said Nadia from 4B.

"You won't eat Milly, Molly and Mac while I draw breath!" Nadia and Ethan's stepdad flung his body over a cage containing three baffled-looking guinea pigs.

"No! That's not what he meant! Rex is harmless. The only thing he might eat by mistake are your sandwiches," said Bigfoot, coming to his rescue.

"And maybe any Cheez Nubbins. They're my favourite," added Rex.

FLUP! FLUP! FLUP!

A sound was coming from outside the tent.

Nadia and Ethan's stepdad looked like he
had more to say, but everyone started rushing
to the exit to see what was going on. As the
noise grew louder, Sandra caught Rex by the
claw and pulled him through the flap. They
stood there, staring up at the sky, where the
sound was coming from.

"I think I can see something!" She pointed
up at the clouds.

"Now that's an entrance!" said Sandra. "How old do you have to be to fly a helicopter?"

The mayor pranced onto the stage next to the hook-a-duck stall and shook hands with Mr Alfreds, the head teacher. He put his hands in the air. "Greetings, little people! Jimmy Prigg is in the house!"

Everyone cheered.

"I'm here to award the prizes for this –" the mayor stopped to pull a piece of paper from his pocket and glanced at it – "school fair! Hang on, where are the prizes?"

As the mayor looked around the stage, Mr Alfreds gave a start. "Oh lord, I left them in the ruddy pet tent."

Rex perked up. Here was the chance to be a helpful PE teacher, instead of appearing to be a pet hater.

"Don't worry, Mr Alfreds! I'll get them!"

Rex sprinted off, making the ground shake.

He burst through the flaps of the tent to the sound of guinea pigs going "weep" and the faint smell of poop. Rex made a "bleurgh" face at them and turned to the prizes.

There were a lot, but he was confident he could carry them in one go.

Easy do—
Oh no!

Rex crashed
into the table. He
watched, stunned,
as all the cages
slid to the floor
and pinged open,
one by one.

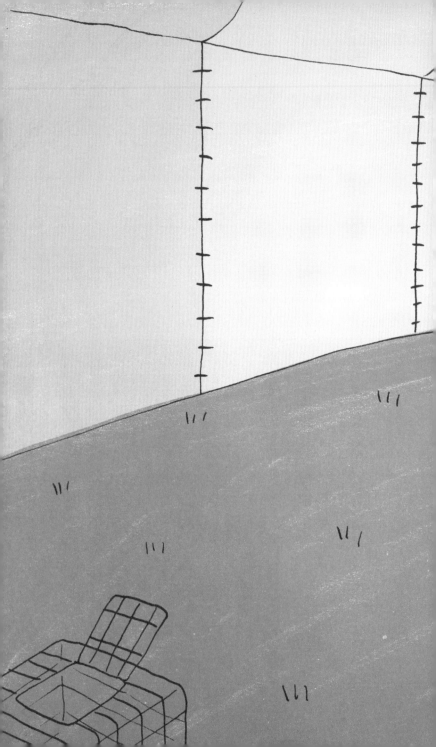

CHAPTER 4
GUINEA PIG EATER

Rex couldn't believe what he was seeing. The guinea pigs had vanished. He frantically searched, but couldn't find a single one.

"Mr Rex! What's taking you so long?" Mr Alfreds marched into the tent, followed by the mayor. Bigfoot, Dodo and all the other parents and children squeezed in behind them.

Anish was silent for a moment as he looked around the tent and then, in an unusually quiet voice, he said, "Rex … where's Mr Fuzzelwuzzelwooo?"

Rex's heart sank. He watched as all the people who knew him – his friends, the other teachers and his neighbours – stared at him. It made his stomach feel uncomfortable, like there was a little storm inside it.

"Isn't it obvious what's happened?" Maddie pushed her way to the front of the crowd. "That creature has eaten them. One by one, like crisps!"

The crowd gasped. Rex moved his mouth up and down as he tried to find the right words. "I didn't eat the gummie pigs; they're mainly poopy fluff!"

"He would deny it! Like I said, you can't trust a monster," said Mr Beaumont, still sweating from the hopping.

Sandra shoved past Mr Beaumont and took Rex by the claw. "There's no proof that Rex's done anything!" she yelled.

"There is proof!" Nadia and Ethan's stepdad shouted from the crowd. "He said that he was going to eat the guinea pigs! I was there."

"That wasn't what I wanted those words to mean!" Rex said.

There was muttering from the crowd.

Rex saw Bigfoot was fiddling with his fur, which he did when he was worried.

"OK." Bigfoot raised his hand to the crowd. "I can see you're all very worried that the guinea pigs are missing, but this had nothing to do with Rex. I can vouch for him."

"Rex is a fine young man ... or a fine old dinosaur, depending on how you look at it," added Mr Dodo with a ruffle of his feathers.

"That's exactly what a monster would say!" Mr Beaumont shoved a group of pet owners aside so he could face the crowd. "You can't trust any of these creatures. They're all liars!"

"Who are you calling a liar, you big bampot?" Nessy folded her flippers.

"You! You spend all day dressed up as a lifeguard, pretending you're some kind of human! A PE teacher! A restaurateur! A…" Mr Beaumont pointed at each one in turn, pausing at Bigfoot.

"A senior printer operator!" said Bigfoot, folding his arms and huffing.

"Yes … that!" Mr Beaumont continued. "You can't trust people who spend all day in disguise, lying about who they really are!"

"That is for my own privacy!" said Nessy. "You have no idea what it's like to be a celebrity."

"ORDER, ORDER!"

Two large figures dressed in dark suits and sunglasses pushed people aside to clear a path. The mayor swanned through the gap to the front.

"I'm sure there's a perfectly reasonable explanation for all this, but are we going to do these prizes or not?" The mayor looked at Mr Alfreds. "I don't have all day. I'm extraordinarily busy and important."

Mr Beaumont strode over to the mayor and prodded him in the chest.

"This community is supposed to be safe for families and small mammals. Are you just going to leave a ravenous dinosaur roaming about while there are vulnerable pets missing?! What if it is children next? Also, I'd like to make a complaint about the outcome of the hopping competition."

The mayor pulled a handkerchief from his pocket and blotted Mr Beaumont's sweaty head.

"There'll be a full enquiry just as soon as I've formed a committee."

"I do enjoy a committee—" started Mr Beaumont.

"I thought you would. Now, that's the end of the matter for today, little people." The mayor stared around the tent. "If you'll excuse me, I'm late for darts with the chief of police. You can keep this."

Maddie squeezed her way over to her father and tugged at his hand. "Daddy, you're not going to let the monster get away with this, are you?" she said.

Mr Beaumont went all pink. "Certainly not, my sugar-plum darling!"

He turned to the rest of the parents. "If there are any responsible members of our community who care about children's safety, follow me!" He stormed out of the tent.

Rex watched a worryingly large number of other parents go after him.

Sandra looked up at Rex and said, "I don't like that guy."

Rex nodded in agreement.

CHAPTER 5
MYSTERY TIME

After the fair finished and they had lunch, Rex, Bigfoot, Sandra and Anish squeezed into Sandra's bedroom. Bigfoot had offered to babysit while Sandra's parents took the triplets to baby gymnastics.

Rex sat on the floor fiddling with his claws. Anish was curled up on the bunk bed with red-rimmed eyes. Sandra looked from one to the other, wondering if there was a way that she could fix this.

"Are you angry at me?" Rex gazed up at Anish with big, sad eyes. "I tried to carry all the prizes but it went wrong, and I don't know where the gwinny pigs went."

Sandra thought that Anish had every right to feel angry. Mr Fuzzelwuzzelwooo was nowhere to be found. But Sandra knew that this wasn't Rex's fault. He'd messed up, that was for sure, but there was something else going on here.

Anish gave a long sigh and looked down at Rex. "I don't think I feel angry, but I do feel sad." Anish hugged his knees. "I know you didn't eat the guinea pigs – that was just Maddie making trouble – but … well … Rex…" Anish sighed again. "There's still so much you get wrong."

Rex stared at his feet and said quietly, "I can try to find out—"

"How are you going to find out what happened to Mr Fuzzelwuzzelwooo when you don't even understand what a pet is? You can't be trusted with something this important, Rex," Anish snapped and then looked shocked at how he sounded.

Rex turned away and put his claws to his face. "Perhaps Maddie's dad is right and I shouldn't be around humans."

"Don't listen to that sweaty fool Mr Beaumont," said Bigfoot. "I know you still find the human world confusing, Rex, but it takes time to understand things. I'm still confused by rollercoasters. I mean, how can they be fun?" Bigfoot put a hand on Rex's shoulder, but

Rex still looked like all the air had been let out of him.

"Sorry, Rex. I know you're trying… I just… I miss Mr Fuzzelwuzzelwooo so much." Anish buried his head in his knees.

Sandra climbed up onto the bunk bed and put an arm around him. "It's OK, Anish. I think we can sort this."

While everyone had been talking, Sandra had been thinking. "You didn't eat the guinea pigs, Rex, so that means that someone has taken them. Don't you see? We have a mystery to solve!"

"Really? Do you think we could get Mr Fuzzelwuzzelwooo back?" Anish lifted his head.

Rex looked a little perkier too. "And find the other gibbly pigs?"

"If we could prove who took the guinea pigs, then everyone would know it wasn't Rex," said Bigfoot, scratching his hairy chin. "Then maybe Maddie's dad will leave us alone. He's trouble, I can sense it in my toes. Yetis have very sensitive toes."

Sandra was getting excited now. She could feel a plan coming. "Yes! And if this thief has a taste for guinea pigs—"

"Not funny, Sandra," said Anish.

"Sorry, didn't think!" Sandra continued. "The thief may well strike again. Are there any other guinea pigs in the neighbourhood?"

"All the pet ones were at the show –" Anish's eyes went wide – "but the city farm has loads! There's a whole pen of them."

Rex jumped to his feet.

"Let's go now! We can't let those ninny pigs be taken too. Everyone will think it was me!" Rex paused to think. "And someone probably loves them as much as Anish loves Mr Fuzzelwuzzelwooo, no matter how bad they smell."

Bigfoot looked at the window and wrinkled his eyebrows. "I'm not sure. It'll be closing soon."

"Don't worry, Bigfoot. We can break in!" Sandra leaped off the bed. "I'll wear my stealth outfit. Come on!"

"That's not what I meant!" Bigfoot followed Sandra out of the room with his hands over his face.

CHAPTER 6
PETS' CORNER

The city farm was closing for the day when Rex, Sandra, Bigfoot and Anish arrived. Luckily, from a distance, Bigfoot looked like a large sheep.

"Pets' Corner is right over there!" Anish pointed. "My uncle used to take me here all the time, until he got into a fight with that goat."

As they got closer to Pets' Corner, Rex recognized a poopy smell. He looked into a pen and saw it was full of guinea pigs, all gathered round a pile of lettuce. They froze the moment they saw Rex and one let out a shrill "weep!"

"Perfect!" said Sandra, surveying the area. "Stake-out time!"

As well as wearing her stealth clothes, Sandra had insisted on bringing her stealth kit.

"Oooh!" said Rex. "Can I borrow a few bits so I can be stealthy too?"

She was already wearing a headset and enthusiastically brandishing a telescope. Rex and Anish trailed behind her, carrying three very heavy bags containing even more kit.

Anish eyed Sandra's kit. "Where did you get all this?"

"Granny got it for me for Christmas," replied Sandra, shoving the telescope at Anish and grabbing some night-vision goggles despite it being daylight. "She's the best."

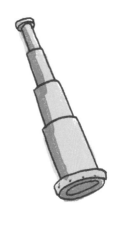

Sandra led them all behind a nearby goat shed. They peered out from behind it, keeping an eye on the guinea pigs.

"What do we do now?" Rex whispered loudly.

"We wait for the thief." Sandra handed Rex a pair of binoculars. "If we can find out who they are, or even capture them, we can prove you are innocent. But stay hidden! We don't want to scare them off."

"We can't be long," said Bigfoot, who settled down

56

beside them. "Your parents will worry if we're out for too long. Do you think there's anywhere round here I can get a coffee?"

But before they had time to figure out how to get Bigfoot a flat white, something happened.

Sandra gasped and flung off her goggles.

"The thief!" she hissed at the others.

Anish clenched his jaw and his fists as, one by one, the guinea pigs began to rise up from the pen. "DON'T YOU TOUCH THOSE GUINEA PIGS!"

Anish leaped to his feet. Sandra tried to grab the back of his shirt but missed. He sprinted towards the guinea pigs and then dived into their pen. But before he hit the ground, something astonishing happened.

"You didn't tell me humans could float!" Rex turned to Bigfoot. "You said it was only balloons."

Bigfoot didn't reply, but ran towards Anish, who was rapidly floating upwards with the guinea pigs.

"Anish, come back! Your mother will kill me!"

Bigfoot jumped higher than Rex imagined

a yeti could and grabbed on to Anish's foot. A look of shock appeared on Bigfoot's face when, instead of pulling Anish down to the ground, he just carried on floating up with him.

Rex and Sandra stared at each other. When they looked back at the sky, Bigfoot and Anish had both disappeared.

"What are we going to do?" Rex gawped down at Sandra.

Sandra never got the chance to answer. Out of nowhere, strong hands grabbed her shoulders. She and Rex were dragged, kicking and struggling, to the exit.

CHAPTER 7
KIDNAP!

Rex and Sandra were flung into the back of a sleek black car waiting outside the farm by silent men wearing dark glasses.

Rex clenched his jaw as he felt the panic starting to build. "Sandra, are they going to lock me up in the zoo again?" he whispered across the car.

Sandra paused and looked around. "I don't think so. It's all a bit too … fancy."

Rex looked at the seat he was sitting on. It was soft and smooth. Through the tinted windows, he noticed that they were in the shiny part of the city that Bigfoot said was for tourists and school trips.

The car squealed round a corner into an underground car park. Rex and Sandra were bundled out of the car and into a lift. They emerged into even fancier surroundings, where the men in dark glasses instructed them to remove their stealth gear and make their way down the corridor.

"Hello, little people! It is I, Jimmy Prigg, your immaculately coiffured overlord – I mean, mayor."

"What's 'a mac-late-crow-fur'?" Rex had no idea what the mayor was talking about.

Sandra slapped her hands on the desk. "Why did you kidnap us? And what's happened to Anish, Bigfoot and the guinea pigs?"

Well, hello!

The mayor slapped his hand on the desk, but harder and louder. "I love bashing things too! If you think the desk is good to bash, you should try bashing it with something breakable like a vase. So many lovely sharp pieces—" The mayor looked dreamily off into the distance before refocusing. "But anyway, let me explain why you're here."

He walked over to the fireplace and stared up at a portrait of himself hanging above it. "You see, I love being mayor. There's this charming office, the elegant cars and secret service agents who do whatever I tell them. Watch. Darren! Do a handstand!"

Without a word, one of the men in dark glasses did a perfect handstand and then hopped back onto his feet.

"Exemplary, Darren!" Jimmy Prigg continued. "And best of all, the little people have to do what I say. This town is mine and

I can play with it how ever I like. Darren, elaborate on some of my awe-inspiring plans!"

"Every day will be Thursday to avoid confusion. All cars will eventually be replaced with ice-cream vans. We are looking into buying France because it seems 'nice'. Mr Prigg will unveil 'The Human Shoot', coming spring next year," barked Darren, while remaining totally expressionless.

Prigg skipped over to a table with a model on it and spread his arms wide.

Rex kneeled to peer at the model. "It's not very big. I think it might work better for mice or large bugs."

"I think it looks dangerous and expensive," said Sandra, folding her arms.

"Oh, it is!" said Prigg, giving her a wink.

The mayor walked over to the desk and flopped down into his chair. He started speaking to Rex and Sandra in the same slow voice Sandra's mum used on Larry, Gary and Barry.

"But you see, I can only be the mayor if the little people want me to be their mayor. They need to vote for me. That means I need happy people who think everything is wonderful. Then they think I'm wonderful – which, clearly, I am. But the reason you are here is because the people aren't happy right now. Do you know why?"

"Is it the rain we've been having?" said Rex.

"Infrastructure issues," said Sandra.

"No." Jimmy Prigg plonked his feet onto the desk and crossed his legs. "Every single guinea pig in this town is missing! People love those weird little furry guys! What's with that?"

"I know!" said Rex.

"The little people are incandescent!"

"In a can-what?" asked Rex.

"IN-CAN-DESCENT!" repeated Prigg. "At the school fair they found someone to blame. Someone who looks different from them. Someone with big teeth and sharp claws."

Rex felt a jolt of panic. He tried to hide his clawed hands behind his back.

"After all –" Prigg came out from behind his desk and put his face very close to Rex's nose – "that sweaty Beaumont man was right. You can't trust someone who goes around in disguise all day."

He turned back to the desk but then whipped around to say, "Do you want to know how I know that? Security, leave us. This is classified."

Rex gulped and waited for the mayor to produce some evidence against him. Instead, Jimmy Prigg started feeling around behind his back.

CLICK!

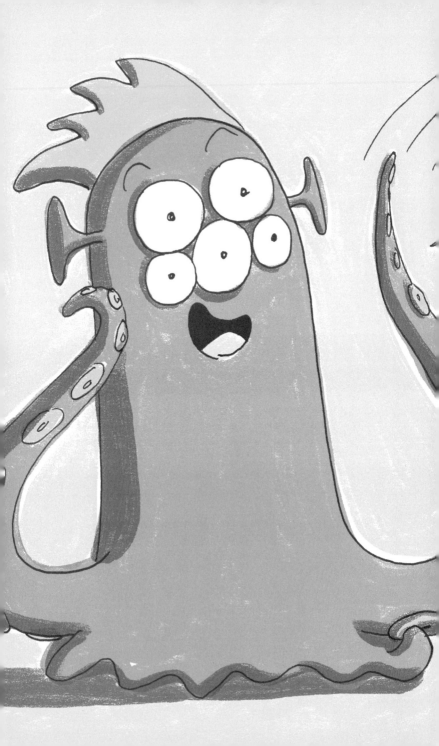

I know you can't trust people in disguise because I'm in disguise – and you definitely can't trust me!

CHAPTER 8
MEET LINDA

Rex stared at the creature standing where the mayor had been. It slithered over to Rex, put a tentacle over his shoulder and whispered into his ear, "I'm very untrustworthy. I always cheat. Especially at darts."

Rex looked over at Sandra and was surprised to see a big smile had appeared on her face.

"You're an alien! I always knew there was life out there!" she said.

Rex's mind was whirring. "So, you're in disguise too? Just like me? Or Bigfoot? Or Nessy and Dodo?"

The alien draped its tentacles over the desk. "The people would never choose me as their mayor. Being in disguise is the only way I could be in charge."

"What's your name?" asked Rex.

"You can call me by my alien name, ☹♓■♎☺."

Rex and Sandra looked blankly at the mayor.

The alien sighed and rolled her eyes. "The closest human translation is 'Linda'. Call me that."

"But how did you get here?" asked Sandra.

"I'm actually from the planet ♏︎♋︎□◆⧚*. Aliens like to visit Earth on holiday. Life on Earth is wild compared to ♏︎♋︎□◆⧚*, you see, so it's a bit like going on a safari. Alien life is all 'We shall all do this exact thing at this exact time in this exact way blah blah blah!' There's no time to break things or make loud noises. But here you've got volcanoes and tigers and sneezing and Cheez Nubbins. It's an enchanting cornucopia of occurrences!"

And have you even seen nail clippers?

"I don't know about the corn-coping but the Cheez Nubbins are great," said Rex.

"Aliens think humans are so wild they consider them an endangered species in the universe," Linda continued. "It's our golden rule that YOU DON'T INTERFERE WITH THE HUMANS."

Sandra narrowed her eyes at Linda. "Isn't being the mayor interfering a little bit?"

"Oh, I don't do rules," said Linda. "I came on holiday but I decided to stay. Normally we land a spaceship on Earth and then disguise ourselves as humans for a week or so. It all adds to the fun, a bit like fancy dress. And humans do tend to freak out when they see an alien – even one as glorious as me."

Linda struck a pose and fluttered her eyelashes. Sandra snorted.

I know, I'm beautiful.

"This city is phenomenal! All you have to do is act charming and promise the humans whatever they want and – BOOM! – you're the mayor with a budget and a limo. No wonder I didn't go home. It's a quagmire from which I never wish to be extricated!"

Rex was trying to take it all in. "So why have you decided to tell us you're an alien? Your disguise is so good even Bigfoot would be impressed."

"Well –" Linda tapped her chin – "I know who's been taking the guinea pigs. Have a look at this."

Linda pulled out a map and unrolled it.

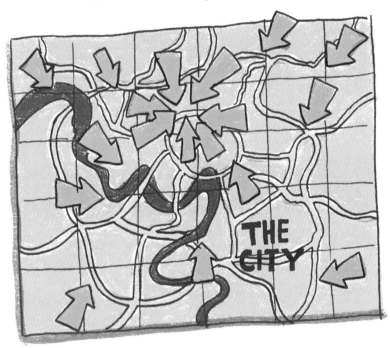

"Guinea pig abductions have been happening all over the country, gradually getting closer to this city. It's the Intergalactic Council, who rule my planet. They're looking for something. And it might be that –" Linda shuffled her tentacles nervously – "the thing they're looking for is … me."

"But you're not a pinny gig; you don't smell the same," said Rex, giving Linda a sniff.

Sandra let out a little gasp. "Oh, I get it. Jimmy Prigg … guinea pig! They've got confused, haven't they?"

"Yep!" giggled Linda. "Those sluggard mini-brains think I'm disguised as a guinea pig. They keeping abducting them, only to discover they're not me. It must be making them apoplectic!"

"But why are they so keen to find you?" asked Sandra.

"Well, apart from the minor interference with humans, I've also got something the Intergalactic Council want. It might also explain why the guinea pig mix-up has happened."

Linda pulled a remote control from her desk drawer. She pointed it at the bookcases, which slid aside to reveal shelves full of objects.

"COOL! Is this all alien stuff?" Sandra ran over and pulled down what looked like a large blaster.

"Yes," said Linda, plucking the blaster out of Sandra's hands. "But they're not looking for this old thing. They're after this."

"That doesn't look very exciting," said Sandra.

"But it is!" Linda was holding the book like it was made of glass. "This is the *Alien–Human Dictionary*. It's the only one in the whole universe. Aliens find human language very confusing."

"But your Human is so good," said Rex. "I can't speak Human like you do!"

"No one speaks Human like she does," said Sandra, who had never heard anyone use the word "quagmire" in a sentence before.

"I brought the dictionary with me on holiday. I've been studying it since I arrived and my human diction is now exemplary. But the Intergalactic Council will be struggling to understand any Human without it."

"Can't they just look the words up online?" said Sandra.

"Oh, there's no alien internet. In fact, they're all baffled why you humans spend so much time looking at your phones. They think you're hypnotized. Anyway, I have a proposition for you."

Linda stuck out two tentacles and pulled Rex and Sandra in close. "Take the dictionary back to the council. It's what they're after. Give them that and they'll release all the guinea pigs they've got captive on their spaceship. Oh, and your friends too."

Sandra struggled out of Linda's grasp.
"Why don't *you* take the dictionary back?
You don't want unhappy people with missing
guinea pigs either."

Linda waggled her tentacles in
the air dramatically. "Me? The
council doesn't care about
me. And anyway, I can't go!
I'm far too busy being the
mayor!"

"You were playing darts
earlier," said Sandra.

"Darts are important!"
Linda turned to Rex with big,
sad eyes. "You'll need to go in
disguise because no humans –
or dinosaurs – are allowed on
the ship. You'll be disguised as
aliens disguised as humans.
It will be elementary for

Pweeze!

someone with your disguise skills, Rex."

Rex didn't even think about it. "It sounds simple. And us creatures have to stick together."

He gave her a hug with his tail and Linda made a "squish" sound.

"Steady there, dino chap. I don't have bones. You'd better get a move on and take the dictionary. The spaceship could head back to ♏︎☉◻◆♒* at any time and that'll be *adios* to your little friends and weird pets."

"Rex, there's something fishy going on here," said Sandra. "All the abductions can't just be because of a dictionary."

"It is a *really* good dictionary, my miniature human friend," said Linda. "Finding the spaceship will be a piece of cake. Just look out for an alien tour group. They'll be disguised as human tourists but, well, sometimes those disguises might be a bit incompetent. They tend to get the time period wrong, and sometimes even the species."

Suddenly, Linda swiped everything off her desk with one of her tentacles and leaped up on it. She scooped her mayor disguise up and started to swish her tentacles back inside in a way that made Rex feel a bit queasy.

"Time for you two to get out of here and solve my problems! And on your way out tell Darren to bring me some vases. I've got some bashing to do."

CHAPTER 9
GOING FOR A COFFEE

The mayor's car bumped up onto the curb and Rex and Sandra were booted out onto the road near to school.

Sandra looked up and down the busy street. "Linda said that we need to find the alien tour group and follow them back to the spaceship."

"But this city is full of tourists," said Rex. "How will we find the right ones?"

Sandra thought about this. "Linda said their touristy human disguises often aren't quite right. Without the dictionary, they probably sound even stranger than Linda. Come on, I know where they'll go if they want an authentic human experience."

Rex followed Sandra to the nearest coffee shop. It wasn't long before they spotted a chattering group of tourists heading towards them, taking up all the pavement.

"Look, Rex!" whispered Sandra, tugging at Rex's sleeve. "That must be them!"

"Are you sure?" said Rex. "They don't look like aliens in disguise to me."

But Sandra had already started towards them. Rex followed and began to listen to their guide.

"Good evening, ladies, gentlemen and undeveloped amoebas! Welcome to tonight's tour of a genuine coffee shop, featuring a bonus demonstration of the excretion capsule known as the toilet!"

The crowd let out a chorus of awed

oooooooOOooooooOOOOOs.

"I shall be speaking in the local dialect for a more authentic experience – apply your earpiece for translation if necessary. Please proceed through the entry flap and place orders for your caffeinated liquids at the service bench."

"Let's follow them!" Sandra grabbed Rex's claw and pulled him inside.

The tourists all queued up to order their coffees. They were chatting loudly and pointing at the displays of paninis and reusable cups. One was taking photographs of a blueberry muffin.

"One high-temperature bean beverage, with the juice of a cow please," said the one who was wearing an **I ♥ Earth** cap.

"And I would like a cow juice with a single portion of bean beverage, but low-temperature, made with the solid H_2O," said the one with the camera.

The baristas looked at each other, puzzled.

"And where are the sweet grains?" said the camera tourist.

"Err, sugar is next to the spoons?" said a barista.

Sandra looked at Rex and Rex had a think.

"I mean, that doesn't seem that alien to me," said Rex. "That person just wanted an iced coffee with sugar, which is a normal human thing to want."

Sandra raised her eyebrows. "How did you get that from what he said?"

"It's obvious, isn't it? It's not more complicated than Bigfoot's coffee order. Are you sure they're aliens?"

"They're clearly suspicious," said Sandra. "Come on, let's gather more evidence."

The suspected aliens took their coffees and sat around the tables. Sandra and Rex squeezed themselves into a squishy sofa in the corner and pretended not to be listening.

"Now that you have your caffeinated liquids," said the guide, "it is customary for patrons to regard their electrical devices. So, if you purchased one at the gift shop, regard it now."

One of the tourists pulled out a laptop and started typing away, just like any normal human. Rex looked round at Sandra and gave her an "I told you so" look. But when he turned

back, he saw a second tourist had produced
and plugged in a microwave and was busy
pressing all the buttons. A third had taken out
an iron and was running it up and down the
table. Now it was Sandra's turn to give Rex an
"I told you so" look.

"Now follow me for the bonus
demonstration of the excretion capsule!"
announced the tour guide.

Half the group got up and followed the
guide over to the single toilet at the back
of the shop and squeezed inside. Rex and
Sandra heard a FLUSH, followed by a loud
"OOOOOooooooh" and a round of applause.

Rex looked down at Sandra. "OK, even I
think that's weird. Maybe you're right."

"No kidding," said Sandra. "Let's follow
them back to their ship, find Anish and Bigfoot
and return the dictionary. Once
they're done in the toilet, that is."

CHAPTER 10
BEAM ME UP

The other shops on the street were starting to close as Rex and Sandra followed the aliens out of the coffee shop into the park where the spaceship was waiting. They were beamed up with the rest of the tour group and then everything seemed to happen at once.

"Woah, these aliens really do make a holiday to Earth look fun," said Rex, looking around inside the ship.

"No wonder Linda wanted to stay on Earth," said Sandra as an alien directed her towards a queue. "Right, Rex, we need a plan. We need to find someone who looks important and can take us to the council so we can return the dictionary."

"What makes you look important?" said Rex.

Sandra thought about this. "A fancy uniform, a tall hat and maybe a big hairstyle or a moustache? And remember that no humans are allowed on the ship. So, you're a dinosaur pretending to be a human who's pretending to be an alien who's pretending to be a human."

Before Rex could work out what he was supposed to be, the queue reached a long bar. Rex saw that there was a moving conveyor belt on the top. On top of the belt were big platters. Rex identified them as being full of FOOD.

"Is this a buffet?" He put his little claws up to his face. "I love a buffet!"

Rex picked up a plate and started spooning food onto it. He turned to Sandra with a big grin on his face. "Bigfoot once took me to the all-you-can-eat buffet in town. It was the best day of my life. What would you like?"

"Err … not that one," said Sandra.

"How about this?"

"I think I'm allergic to that."

"Now this looks delicious!"

"Do you know what, I don't think I'm hungry."

Rex shrugged and started tucking in. "You don't know what you're missing."

Sandra turned away from the conveyor belt and looked around the room. "We can't be distracted by an intergalactic buffet, Rex. We need to find someone who can take us to the council."

Rex was finding the buffet irresistible. "The food reminds me of prehistoric times! If I didn't know better, I'd say this was megalodon sushi…"

There was no reply. Sandra wasn't by his

side. She was walking across the room to an important-looking alien in a hat, holding out the dictionary. The alien started yelling and waving its tentacles. All the other aliens in the room turned to see what was happening.

A line of security aliens marched into the buffet area and grabbed Sandra with their tentacles. One of them plucked the dictionary out of her hand and another looked at the back of her neck.

"This being is not alien. There is no disguise applied to its form. It is HUMAN! Initiate human protocol! EJECT IT FROM THE SHIP!"

The aliens dragged Sandra towards a hatch in the wall.

"But I thought the council wanted the dictionary!" Sandra was fighting against the tentacles that were squeezing her tight.

Rex knew he had to do something to stop

Sandra falling back to Earth. He looked down at his plate and grabbed a piece of food.

The security aliens froze, but it seemed to give all the tourists ideas.

Rex was starting to enjoy himself when a loud voice shouted, "WHAT IS THE OCCURRENCE HERE!? THIS IS SUPPOSED TO BE AN ORGANIZED VACATION!"

The aliens froze.

Rex looked over to see where the voice had come from and was confronted by an alien who really did look important.

"⚐□◆■◍⟊●●□□ ⚐⟊■■⟊⬧!" said one of the guards, who had managed to catch Sandra by the ankle.

"Talk Human please," said the important alien. "We must practise for greater skills."

"Mighty Councillor Much-Paper!" the guard started again. "That alien started a sandwich war!"

The guard pointed at Rex. Rex looked around innocently.

"And a human

has intruded the ship!" He held Sandra up by one leg. "It has the dictionary! We were about to eject it."

Councillor Much-Paper dropped to what passed for knees at the sight of the dictionary.

"It is recovered! Do not eject that human! We must take her to THE BOSSY BOSS! And bring Mr Sandwich War too. He is clearly a punishable mess."

Security rushed towards Rex and started dragging him out of the room by the tail.

"But –" Rex shouted – "what about dessert?!"

CHAPTER 11
FANCY PANTS

Sandra and Rex were escorted by the security aliens through the ship until they stopped in front of a big door. It slid open and Rex was confronted by quite a sight.

Rex was taken to the side of the room. The guards dropped Sandra in front of the biggest alien. Councillor Much-Paper then handed her the dictionary and bowed. She waggled her tentacles in delight.

The big alien looked at Sandra. "Human! Tremble in afraid because I am ↗︎☾■♍⌂ ▢☾■♦•, the shiny and spectacular head of the Intergalactic Council!"

Sandra looked back at her. "You're who?"

The big alien sighed. "The nearest human translation is – " she flicked through the dictionary – "Fancy Pants!"

Sandra stifled a laugh.

"What?!" said Fancy Pants.

"Nothing, Fancy Pants," said Sandra.

"HUMAN! How did this become for you?" The alien waved the dictionary.

"Linda asked me to return it and she didn't say you'd be so rude about it!"

All the aliens gasped. Fancy Pants clenched her tentacles and went a sort of purple colour.

"Do not mention the name of Linda! She has smashed intergalactic law by stealing this dictionary and staying on Earth, unauthorized. She also said very hurtful things about myself! Bring me Linda's last crop circle."

"Crop circle?" said Sandra.

"It is the alien way of sending messages." Fancy Pants gestured and an alien with a big hat passed her a photo of a field. She began to read it out.

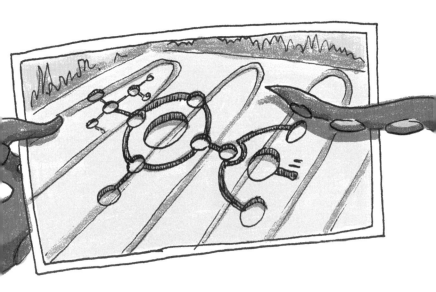

Dear Alien Losers,

It's me, Linda! I want to let you know that I'm staying on Earth. Fancy Pants, you've been bossing me around since school, but now you keep your stubby tentacles out of my business or I'll stick them up your excretion tube! I'm a better Jimmy Prigg than you'll ever be.

So long, Sticky Tentacles!

PS You don't know it, but when you laugh, slime comes out.

"That is quite rude," said Rex. The guard beside him flicked Rex with his tentacle.

"Slime does not come out when I laugh!" yelled Fancy Pants. "I do not laugh."

The alien coughed and readjusted her big hat.

"Linda has snapped intergalactic law and must be given punishment! I will not sit down until I see her captured! But Linda's dysfunctional brain has passed me the advantage. She told us her disguise! I just need to obtain the correct Jimmy Prigg. I have searched Earth, but she still evades me. I do not understand why Linda wants to live with humans disguised as an excretion-scented hair ball, but she is not a usual alien."

"She also isn't a usual human," said Sandra and sighed. "I think you might have got your tentacles all tangled up, so to speak. Linda said she's *Jimmy Prigg*. That's a human name. You're thinking of a *guinea pig* – those are the hairy ball creatures."

Fancy Pants furrowed her brow and scowled at Sandra. "How dare you suggest I am incorrect! You regard here…"

Fancy Pants had been flicking through the dictionary but came to a sudden stop.

GUINEA PIG

A spherical animal that acts as a companion to humans. It consumes lettuce and fears eagles, loud noises and most movements.

"Oh … right … it is titled 'guinea pig' … I, umm … I was sure…" Fancy Pants looked down at the other council members; one stifled a giggle.

The big alien went a bit pink round the face, but then clutched the dictionary tight and her anger seemed to return, bigger than ever.

"When I get my tentacles on Linda, she will be placed on cleaning duty on Pluto for a minimum of three millennia and receive an all-life ban from Earth! If you are Linda's friend, you're an enemy of mine." Fancy Pants pointed at Sandra. "Security! Take her to the containment centre with the other Jimmy Priggs and Earth beings. I shall deal with her later. Next bring forward the buffet vandal!"

CHAPTER 12
EATS MANY CRISPS

Rex tried to wave at Sandra as she was dragged out of the room, but the guards pulled him in front of Fancy Pants.

The big alien leaned down towards Rex and said, "⚇☿☉♦ ⽊♦ ♦☿⽊♏ ☉♏☉■⽊■Ⅴ ◻⤬ ♦☿⽊♦?!"

Rex stared at her with his mouth a little open. Sandra hadn't told him what to do in this situation. "Umm … sorry? I don't understand. Can you say that in Human?"

Fancy Pants rolled her eyes and said, "Who are you and why did you begin a sandwich war in the buffet area? This is an organized holiday!"

Rex thought about this. If he could pretend to be a human, how hard could it be to pretend to be an alien?

"It was an accident! I was a bit umm … shocked by the human in the buffet, you know, because I'm an alien and I know humans are not allowed on spaceships. I threw my food in surprise. I'm very sorry. I agree mess-making is not good."

Rex clasped his claws, trying not to fidget. He looked Fancy Pants in the eye. She raised an eyebrow.

"I'm a regular alien. I love these." Rex held up one of the tentacle snacks from the buffet.

Some of the other aliens nodded.

Fancy Pants folded her tentacles. "Then how come your only good speak is Human, not Alien?"

"Oh, I'm not from your planet. I'm from a different one called –" Rex stuck out his tongue and made his thinking face – "Super-Awesome Prehistoric Cheez Nubbins Fun Town."

"I've never been," said Fancy Pants.

"Oh, it's from a very long time ago …
I mean … far away. We speak differently
to you. In my language my name is
RRROOOAOAOOAOOAAR!" Rex gave a
big roar and then wiped the spit from a nearby
guard who'd been in the wrong place at the
wrong time. "Which in Human translates to …
um … Eats Many Crisps!"

"How did you come to be on my ship, Eats Many Crisps?"

"I ended up in the human world by mistake. I got frozen and then when I unfroze, I was in the city."

"Space is cold," said Fancy Pants.

"I've been disguised as a human for a while now. But then I found out you aliens were in town. I joined your tour group and … here I am."

Fancy Pants nodded wisely. "You have done super excellent to survive this time, Eats Many Crisps. No wonder you started a sandwich war when you saw a human intruder. They are confusing and unpredictable beings."

Rex nodded frantically in agreement.

There was chattering from the rest of the council. An official-looking alien warily slid up to Rex and took a good look at him.

"Excellent shiny leader," the alien said to

Fancy Pants, "could the creature's good Human speak but weird looks be because he is not an alien, but the ancient Earth creature known as the dinosaur?"

Fancy Pants rolled her eyes. "Don't be fool-like. Dinosaurs don't exist. They are just night-time stories constructed to make afraid human children."

"Exactly," said Rex. "We definitely never existed. And I must be an alien – look at my tentacle." Rex turned round and waggled his tail.

Fancy Pants squinted at Rex. "Pointy teeth, vibrant colour and a single tentacle. And just look at what he's wearing! This is no Earth human. I can only conclude that Eats Many Crisps must be alien."

Rex thought he was wearing one of his better human outfits today, but he decided not to complain.

Fancy Pants continued, "We shall return you to your planet once we have returned the tourists. Until then, you must clear the food debacle you created in the buffet zone."

Fancy Pants snapped a tentacle and one of the guard aliens gave Rex a bucket and mop.

"Begone!" Fancy Pants waved. "I do not want to return without my Linda revenge, but the tourists' holiday is over. I shall go to the cockpit to set a course for home."

Two guard aliens took Rex by the arms and pushed him out of the door. It swooshed shut behind him and he was left alone with his bucket. Rex set off down the corridor, but he wasn't off to mop up. Rex was on a rescue mission.

CHAPTER 13
INTERGALACTIC CLEANER

Rex didn't know where to start looking for his friends on the spaceship, so he had taken a trial-and-error approach.

He knocked on the door of every room he could find. But there was no sign of Sandra, Anish, Bigfoot or the guinea pigs. Just as he was wondering what to do next, he got lucky.

He opened a door and saw what looked like a very deep but empty swimming pool. Rex could hear familiar voices – and lots of "weep!" "weep!" noises – coming from the bottom.

"OK, I've got another escape idea…" That sounded like Sandra.

"Does it involve challenging the aliens to single combat again?" And that could be Anish.

"Yes, but—"

Rex lay down on his belly and stuck his head over the edge.

"Hi, guys!" Rex waved down at them.

Sandra leaped to her feet. "You made it, Rex! What happened?"

"I'm still in disguise! They think I'm some kind of weird alien. The one with the fancy pants gave me a bucket and now they think I work here."

"Good job, Rex! You're a master of disguise now!" Anish called up to him.

"And you're a hero!" Rex shouted back. "You tried to save those giddy pigs back at the farm single-handed."

"Thanks. I take guinea pig safety very seriously," said Anish. "But we're not saved yet. Everyone's stuck down here."

Anish pointed to Bigfoot, who was sat next to him surrounded by hundreds of guinea pigs.

"Wait, is that your gifty pig?" said Rex, pointing at something on Anish's shoulder.

"Yes, I've got Mr Fuzzelwuzzelwooo back!" said Anish, giving him a cuddle. "And everyone else's guinea pig too."

Bigfoot stood up and looked down at one of the guinea pigs, who was nibbling at his fur. "I'm delighted to see you, Rex, but there's no time for dramatic reunions. We've got to find a way out of here soon. I think the guinea pigs are hungry."

"It might be tricky, Bigfoot," said Rex. "Has Sandra told you what happened with Linda, the dictionary and the alien council?" asked Rex.

Bigfoot and Anish nodded.

"I don't understand why Linda said that if we gave the dictionary back the aliens would let you all go. Fancy Pants seems very angry," said Rex.

"Linda lied," said Anish. "She must have known the aliens were looking for her, but thought that getting the dictionary back might be enough to make them leave her alone."

"Or Linda thought this would happen and wasn't too bothered as long as it wasn't her on this ship," said Sandra. "I knew we couldn't trust her!"

"She sounds like a piece of work," said Anish. "But we still need to get these guinea pigs home. Sandra, tell Rex your plan."

"Hmm." Sandra rubbed her chin. "I haven't figured out all the details, but we could stand on Bigfoot's shoulders and climb out, then I'll defeat Fancy Pants in single combat and we can take control of the ship!"

Rex thought Sandra's plan sounded very exciting, but Anish seemed to think it needed double-checking.

"This pool is so deep that even if we

all stood on each other's shoulders, we still wouldn't reach the top, and then how would we get Bigfoot out?" Anish asked. "I know you'd be terrifying in single combat, but we probably shouldn't start a battle. My mum would be furious if that happened. And we don't know how to drive a spaceship."

"It can't be that different from a car," said Sandra.

"We don't know how to drive one of those either," said Anish.

"What's important is that we make it back to Earth and don't end up on ♏︎☌□◆♒︎*," said Bigfoot. "Otherwise, we'll be in real trouble."

"That's excellent alien pronunciation," Anish said to Bigfoot.

"Thank you. I've had some time to practise. Rex, can you pull us out?"

Bigfoot went to the side of the pool. Sandra and Anish climbed up onto Bigfoot's hairy shoulders and Rex stretched his little arms down towards them. Even when they all stretched as high as they could, Rex still couldn't reach them.

Rex dangled his head over the edge as the others slumped back down into the pool.

"Don't worry, Rex," said Sandra. "We can find a way out of here. The tricky thing is getting this ship back down to Earth. How do you think you control it?"

A light went on in Rex's head. "I think I know how to do that! Fancy Pants said there's a place called the armpit where you can set a course for home!" He leaped to his feet and started for the door.

"Rex! Are you sure that's right?" Bigfoot called after him.

"Wait!" shouted Anish. "At least save Mr Fuzzelwuzzelwooo! He's never gone this long without lettuce before. Get ready."

Anish braced himself and, as carefully as he could, tossed the guinea pig up into Rex's arms. Rex stiffened as he caught the guinea pig, expecting to get bitten, but instead Mr Fuzzelwuzzelwooo just gave a confused little "squeee" and snuggled into Rex's shoulder. Rex gave him a tentative stroke.

"OK, don't worry, guys. I have a plan." Rex carefully hid Mr Fuzzelwuzzelwooo in his bucket and slipped out of the room.

"Do you think Rex is our only hope of getting home?" Bigfoot asked Sandra.

"Unless you want me to enter into single combat," said Sandra.

Bigfoot put his head in his hands. "Oh, goodness me."

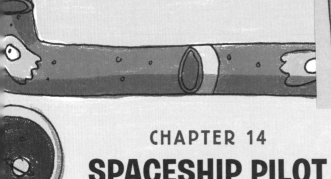

CHAPTER 14
SPACESHIP PILOT

Back in the ship's corridors, Rex knew where he needed to go, but not where it was. Fortunately, the aliens were pretty helpful when they thought you were one of them.

Once Rex had found the right door, he lifted the bucket to his face and whispered inside, "You're doing really well in this bucket disguise, Mr Fuzzelwuzzelwooo. Now all we've got to do is fly this ship back to Earth. It can't be much different from taking the bus, can it?"

Mr Fuzzelwuzzelwooo said, "Weep!"

"OK, here we go." Rex pressed the button and the doors whooshed open.

"This is more complicated than I thought," Rex said into the bucket, trying to take it all in.

"What do you want?" said the alien sitting at the controls, picking up a cup.

"I'm the cleaner!" said Rex, lifting his bucket, which said, "Weep!"

Rex ignored the bucket. "I'm here to clean up the mess. Is it just you here?"

"The other crew are on their beverage consumption break, so just I must view the controls for security. There is mess here and it makes me feel dislike."

"OK! I'm on it!"

Rex went over to the mess and started mopping at it.

"I think that desk is probably the one that controls the ship as it has a big handle. We need to get over there," Rex whispered to the bucket and pointed at the biggest control panel.

Rex started to creep over to the controls. Just before he got there, the alien made him jump.

"That is not the mess area!" he said, sounding annoyed. "Please return to the mess and complete your duties!"

"Oh, sorry! I just thought I'd give it a dust."

Rex tiptoed back over to his bucket. Once the alien wasn't looking, he whispered into it. "The alien will notice if I go near the controls again. But he'll never spot you, Mr Fuzzelwuzzelwooo! You're small. Do you think you can drive this thing?"

Mr Fuzzelwuzzelwooo looked up at Rex from the bucket and said, "Weep!"

"That sounds like a yes," said Rex.

He carefully lifted the guinea pig out and placed him on the floor. Mr Fuzzelwuzzelwooo's eyes went wide, and he hid behind the bucket.

"OK," said Rex. "Maybe you need some motivation."

Rex felt around in his pocket and pulled out three somewhat fluffy Cheez Nubbins. He showed them to Mr Fuzzelwuzzelwooo, whose nose twitched excitedly.

"If you want them, they'll be over there." Rex threw the Nubbins and they landed just beyond the big handle on the control panel.

At the sight of food, Mr Fuzzelwuzzelwooo became a different guinea pig. He was off like a shot across the cockpit, climbed onto the console and then made a dive for the control panel where the Nubbins had landed.

Unluckily for Mr Fuzzelwuzzelwooo though, he got stuck along the way.

CHAPTER 15
BUM CRAC

Back on Earth, it was getting dark. Nessy hurried towards Dodo Burger as fast as her flippers would carry her. She burst through the doors and slammed them behind her.

"I've just turned off the fryers, Nessy—"

"I'm not interested in burgers, Dodo. There's trouble coming and we need to be ready!"

Dodo waddled over to the window and peered outside. He didn't like what he saw.

"Hang on," said Dodo. "Does that spell—"

"Aye, it does," said Nessy. "But that's not important right now. What's important is that this bunch of scunners chased me here from the leisure centre and they don't seem very friendly towards the likes of me and you."

"I knew this day would come!" Dodo hopped off the table. "The humans ate my ancestors, and now they've come for me! I thought if I kept them full of quality fast food, they'd leave me alone, but you know humans. Well, I'm not going down without a fight!"

Dodo started pulling metal shutters over the windows and door and padlocking them.

By now they could hear the mob chanting outside.

"DELETE THE DINOSAURS! BAN THE BIGFOOTS! DISMISS THE DODOS! NESSIES ARE A NO-NO! SAVE OUR GUINEA PIGS! SAVE OUR CITY!"

"I cannae help but take this personally," said Nessy.

BANG BANG BANG! Someone was knocking on the door.

"We demand you come out right now!" It was Mr Beaumont.

Dodo went over to the door, slid open a little hatch in the metal shutter and yelled, "We're closed!"

Mr Beaumont continued, "As the elected representative of the Community Rally Against Creatures ..."

"We didn't elect you!" came a voice from the back.

He ignored that. "... we demand that you come out so we can hand you over to the proper authorities."

"Which is the zoo!" added Maddie from behind her father's legs.

"Why would we do that then?" Nessy yelled through the hatch.

"Because you're a menace to the local community!" Mr Beaumont waved his placard.

"The only thing menacing about me is my uncanny flair for business!" shouted Dodo. "Totter off, BUM CRAC, or I'm getting the ketchup!"

Mr Beaumont didn't seem threatened by ketchup. "Your dinosaur friend has been eating our pets, and we're going to put a stop to it now. Clearly it isn't safe to  have creatures like you living in a human neighbourhood, especially an upscale one like this!"

"I'm calling my lawyer!" yelled Dodo.

"Rex hasn't been eating your furry wee pets. You've got no proof because it didnae happen," said Nessy.

Mr Beaumont puffed out his chest. "No proof, you say? Maddie, my sugar-plum darling, tell them what you saw."

Maddie stepped forward and said, "I saw him do it! He ate them, one after another, just like he does with Cheez Nubbins!"

"That's a bold lie, you little stirrer!" shouted Nessy. "You cannae believe this tripe?"

Maddie's performance was interrupted by Sandra's mum and dad, complete with triple buggy, pushing their way up to the door, followed by Anish's mum.

Sandra's mum spoke through the hatch. "Nessy? Dodo? Have you seen Sandra and Anish?"

"Bigfoot was babysitting, but when I came to pick Anish up, no one was there," added Anish's mum.

"I've not seen them since I got back to my affordable but delicious restaurant, Mrs S," said Dodo.

"Did you hear that!" yelled Maddie. "Now they're taking us children! He must have

EATEN Sandra and Anish too. Sandra was my best friend!"

"That's not what we think…" said Sandra's dad, but this time Maddie managed to produce some actual fake tears. The Hannahs ran out of the crowd and started comforting her.

Mr Beaumont took the bait. "Eating children is the last straw! If you monsters don't come out, we're going to break down that door!"

Inside, Dodo looked at Nessy. "We're going to need some more locks, Ness."

Nessy sighed, but then something caught her eye through the hatch. "Hang on a minute, what's that up in the sky? It's coming straight for us!"

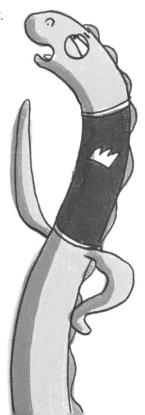

CHAPTER 16
ALIEN INVASION

Rex popped open the escape hatch in the cockpit and slid down the side of the ship, still holding his bucket.

He spotted the crowd outside Dodo Burger. "Sorry about the landing. I don't think Mr Fuzzelwuzzelwooo actually knows how to drive."

The guinea pig popped its head over the edge of the bucket and said, "Weep!"

Mr Beaumont swung around and stared at the wreckage of the spaceship. The look on his face made Rex think that something might have short-circuited in his head.

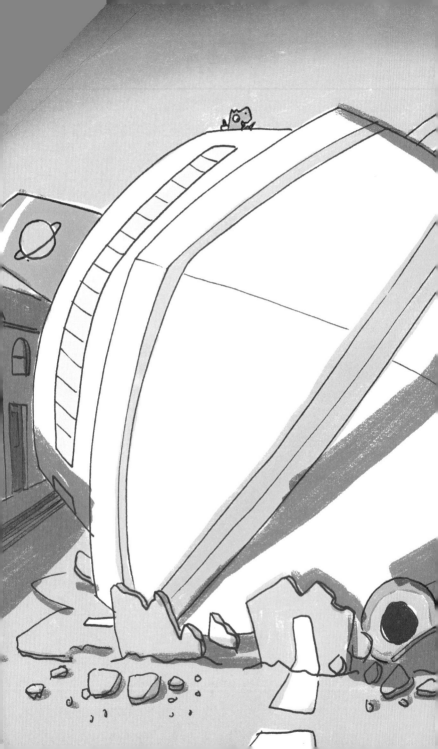

"Do ... do ... do you even have a licence for that thing? And you've parked it across the double yellows—"

He was silenced when a much larger hatch opened and out poured lines of aliens.

"Yetis and guinea pigs first!" shouted Sandra, as she, Anish and Bigfoot burst out of the hatch, followed by a whole herd of guinea pigs.

Rex stood on his tiptoes and waved. "How did you guys escape?"

"It was easy to get out of that pool once it was turned sideways," Sandra shouted, pointing at the upended ship.

"Is Mr Fuzzelwuzzelwooo OK?" Anish called.

Rex held up his bucket and gave a claws up. The crowd of parents and children rushed towards their missing guinea pigs. This did not please Mr Beaumont.

"Don't approach those creatures, CRAC members! We might have been mistaken about the guinea pig eating, but they've still damaged our street and brought all these –" he gestured wildly at the aliens – "foreigners to our neighbourhood!"

"Oh, these guys are no problem!" Rex called, pointing at the lines of tourists as he slid down the side of the ship to join the others.

He didn't get the chance to say anything else because there was a thumping behind him. Rex turned to see some very different aliens making their way out of the ship.

"Oh, that one might be a problem though," said Rex.

Fancy Pants boomed orders to the guard aliens. They spread out and started to surround the group of parents, children and guinea pigs.

"It's an invasion!" yelled Mr Beaumont. "Get behind me, my delicate vase!"

He pushed Maddie behind his back. He was shoved out of the way as Sandra's parents charged towards their daughter.

"Sandra Shellman!" said her mum. "Don't you tell me you've become involved in an alien invasion!"

"Um, I didn't mean to," said Sandra, who bent down to say hi to her baby brothers.

"Earth humans!" came Fancy Pants' voice over the crowd. "My ship it is down-side up! This is an act of war and you are a bad nuisance to the rest of the galaxy! I've had enough. If you will not tell to me the place of hiding of the alien known as Linda, I shall commandeer this planet."

There was a muttering in the human crowd.

"Who's Linda?"

"Is that Linda from the hairdresser's?"

"No, she's in the Algarve this time of year."

Sandra made her way to Rex. "Shall we just tell Fancy Pants that Linda's the mayor and get this over with?"

Rex started and looked down at Sandra. "We can't reveal another undercover creature! That's what Maddie did to me."

"Linda did lie to us about what would happen on that ship. And she only uses her disguise to get what she wants, like being in charge and having a limo."

Rex furrowed his brow. "Yes, Linda is sort of not great, but she's come to this city and is trying to live her human life, just like me or Bigfoot or Nessy or Dodo. I can't just let Fancy Pants take that away from her. Linda's one of us."

"There are quite a lot of aliens over there who might disagree," said Sandra, pointing at the guards that were gradually surrounding them.

CHAPTER 17
SINGLE COMBAT

Sandra was starting to wonder if Rex had a point when a line of fancy black cars came tearing around the corner. Linda, disguised as Jimmy Prigg, jumped out, followed by her secret service agents.

"What's all this I hear about a BUM CRAC outside Dodo Burger..." But then Linda turned and saw the spaceship on the street and all the aliens. "No, Rex! Sandra! You were supposed to return that dictionary, not start an interplanetary conflict! Now I'm going to have to clean up your mess."

Linda started walking towards Fancy Pants with her arms held in the air. She stopped in front of the much bigger alien and said, "Hi, ♦︎⚏︎♍︎◻︎♍︎, ☞︎☺︎■︎♍︎⌂ ▷︎☺︎■︎♦︎•︎✌ ✺︎♦︎• ◯︎♍︎⌨ Linda! ✺︎⑂⚎ ⌂◻︎♦︎ ◯︎⑂•• ◯︎♍︎?"

Fancy Pants let out a roar and waved her tentacles in the air. *She clearly hasn't let go of that slime comment*, thought Sandra.

Linda kept talking, "✺︎ &;■︎◻︎• ⌂◻︎♦︎'◻︎♍︎ ◯︎☺︎⚎ ♌︎♦︎♦︎ ✺︎ Earth. ✺︎'◯︎ ♦︎⚏︎♍︎ ●︎♍︎☺︎⚎♍︎◻︎/mayor •︎⚏︎⑂♍︎⚏︎ ⑂• fun ☺︎■︎⚎ ♦︎⚏︎♍︎◻︎♍︎• ☺︎◯︎☺︎✲⑂■︎♑ ♦︎⚏︎⑂■︎&;• ●︎⑂&;♍︎ limousines, iced lattes, ☺︎■︎⚎ fire!"

The crowd silently watched as their mayor communicated with a huge tentacled alien.

"What do you think they're talking about?" Rex whispered to Sandra.

"I'm not totally sure, but I think Linda is trying to convince Fancy Pants why she should stay."

Fancy Pants gave a low laugh and said, "Hi,
◆□⊬⌂ ●⊬◆◆●⋔ ⊙⊬■⌂⚲. ⊕⋔ ⋔⚲■'◆ ●⋔⚲❖⋔
⊡□◆ ⊬■ ⋔⚲⌐⊙⊓⋔ □↗ ◆≈⊬⋅ □●⚲■⋔◆. ✋ ◆⊬●
≈⚲❖⋔ ◆□ ◆⚲&⋔ □❖⋔□."

At this Linda clenched her fists and started
to yell in Human.

"I haven't destroyed human society, look!"
She pointed at Dodo Burger and Mike's News
and Lotto next door. "This place is a paradise!
I'm the best human mayor these little people
have ever seen and I've not even opened the

Human Shoot yet!
You always took
all my toys,
Fancy Pants,
even when we
were just eggs,
and now you
think you can
take my city

too because you're having a bit of a hissy fit? Well, it's not my fault you don't know what a guinea pig is and you speak Human like an unintellectual, discombobulated ...

BUMFACE!"

Fancy Pants went a shade of hot pink. "You are only good because you are a dictionary stealer!"

Fancy Pants turned to the rest of the crowd. "Humans of Earth! This Jimmy Prigg is criminal and not fit to be your overlord! As head of the Intergalactic Council, I have authority to take over this planet! Unless ... there is an alien here who can beat me in single combat to become the new head of the Intergalactic Council! But if they lose, they will be served at tomorrow's buffet."

Fancy Pants turned to Linda and gave her an evil smile. "My Human talk may not be of high standard, but my single combat is the tallest."

Sandra's mouth opened wide, and she looked at Anish. "I told you single combat was a good plan! It's always a good plan."

"I don't think you can say it always is," said Anish.

Linda suddenly looked around as if she didn't know what to do. Fancy Pants drew herself up to her full size and loomed over Linda.

"You cannot beat me in your pathetic human form. Remove your disguise!"

The humans in the crowd were looking around at each other, confused, but the aliens gathered around in the circle and began chanting, "☞✋👌👎❄! ☞✋👌👎❄! ☞✋👌👎❄!"

Linda reached for the zip at the back of her suit. Sandra grabbed Rex's arm. "If Linda takes off that disguise, that's the end of Jimmy Prigg."

Rex squeezed Sandra's arm back and then started walking towards Fancy Pants. "I challenge you to single combat! I'm an alien, remember. Look at my tentacle!" Rex bent over and waggled his tail.

"Rex! Are you sure this is a good idea?"

Bigfoot moved towards Rex but was stopped by two alien guards.

Rex hadn't got into a fight since prehistoric times, and even then it was just with a velociraptor. But Linda didn't stand a chance against Fancy Pants.

Linda scurried over to Rex and gave him a pat on the shoulder. "Thanks, my fine dinosaur friend. You look like you have this situation under control, so I'll, err, just go and stand over there…" Linda tried to sidle back to her limo, but she was stopped by the guards.

Fancy Pants turned her attention towards Rex. "Eats Many Crisps! You challenge me? Fine, I shall make you lose. Let battle begin!"

I will fight you with this!

CHAPTER 18
RULER OF THE UNIVERSE

Fancy Pants threw her tentacles in the air and started making a "wjoop wjoop wjoop" noise. All the aliens did the same back, and a couple of parents joined in too, which made Rex wonder whose side they were on. She then slammed her tentacles on the ground and assumed what looked to Rex like a fighting stance.

Rex turned to face her and held his bucket in the air. He let out a big roar, ready for a fight, but Fancy Pants took Rex by surprise.

MY NOSE! It's on my nose! I yield! Just get the Jimmy Prigg off me!

Anish broke away from the crowd and tentatively approached Mr Fuzzelwuzzelwooo. He pulled a Cheez Nubbin from his pocket. At this, Mr Fuzzelwuzzelwooo's nose twitched and he let go of Fancy Pants, hopping into Anish's arms.

Rex looked around feeling stunned. "Does this mean I'm the winner?"

"No!" said Sandra, running up to him. "Mr Fuzzelwuzzelwooo is!"

"All hail the council leader!" The aliens, including Fancy Pants, spread their tentacles on the ground, bowing to the guinea pig.

Councillor Much-Paper scuttled over, bowed and said, "What is your command, mighty intergalactic leader?"

HAIL THE JIMMY PRIGG!

"Weep!" said Mr Fuzzelwuzzelwooo.

"I'll translate!" Linda, her mayor disguise intact, was speed-walking over. "So, the great and wise leader of the Intergalactic Council, Mr Fuzzelwuzzelwooo, declares that you should let me stay here because I'm the best mayor he could possibly imagine."

Anish narrowed his eyes and gave her a poke. "Is there something else?"

"Oh yes!" said Linda. "You should release all the guinea pigs and humans you abducted and go home because you've been a lot of trouble, and I don't need this right now. That's all Mr Fuzzelwuzzelwooo has to say." Linda gave them a wave. "Bye-bye!"

"Weep," said Mr Fuzzelwuzzelwooo.

"Your wish is our command, oh glorious leader." Fancy Pants bowed to the guinea pig and started back to the ship, followed by the other aliens, who began to right their ship, ready to leave.

The parents looked around at each other silently. The moment was broken by Mr Beaumont.

"Mr Mayor! This is all well and good but what are you going to do about the dangerous dinosaur! You can't allow him to walk around the city disguised as a human!"

Linda spun around to face him. "Don't you see, you sweaty little man? The dinosaur saved us from an alien invasion! No one wants to be ruled by an alien overlord, do they?" Linda turned to Rex and gave him a wink. "Not a boring one, anyway! It's only because of Rex and his disguise skills and his guinea pig friend that you're not alien toast."

Linda pulled Rex to his feet. "In fact, for acts of slightly silly bravery, I'm going to award Rex the key to the city!" Linda fumbled in her pocket and handed Rex a key. "Give him a round of applause!"

The surrounding parents started clapping; some even gave a cheer.

"Is this a car key?" said Rex.

"Yes," Linda whispered. "It's for my limo and I'll need it back in a minute."

The only parent who wasn't satisfied was Mr Beaumont, who went bright purple and started shaking. "I'll have to handle this myself! Stand back, Madeleine!" He grabbed a placard from one of the other BUM CRAC members, and looked as if he was about to use it to swat Rex like a fly.

Before Rex could react, a furry bundle leaped out of Anish's arms towards Mr Beaumont.

Rex smiled as he watched the two of them run round and round. "Maybe guinea pigs aren't so bad after all."

CALL THIS CREATURE OFF!

It's n...
bu...

EPILOGUE

A few days after the aliens left, Rex, Sandra and Anish were walking home from school together when they felt strong hands grab their shoulders. They were hauled into a big black car. After a short drive the three of them were led into the mayor's office, with Sandra looking super annoyed.

"SURPRISE! PIZZA PARTY!" yelled Linda, tentacles waving multiple slices of pizza around and covering the wall in pepperoni.

"You don't have to kidnap us every time you want to chat, Linda!" said Sandra, red-faced. "That's the second time this week."

"Oh, hi, guys!" Rex had spotted Bigfoot, Dodo and Nessy eating pizza behind Linda's desk.

"Did she kidnap you too?" asked Sandra.

"No," said Bigfoot. "Linda put a message in our WhatsUp group."

"You guys have a WhatsUp group?" said Rex, wondering what one was and how he could get one.

"Yeah, but it's very boring. Bigfoot just uses it to complain to me about bus timetables, YAWN…" Linda put a tentacle around Rex, Sandra and Anish's shoulders and led them over to a sofa.

"So, how's that guinea pig of yours getting on, Anish?" said Linda.

Anish perked up. "Oh, well, he's pretty much ruler of the universe now he's leader of the Intergalactic Council. He still lives with me in his hutch most of the time, but occasionally the aliens pick him up for a trip to ♍︎♋︎♓︎♦︎♒︎*, where he's very, very popular. Look, they sent me a photo."

Linda glanced at the picture. "He can't be worse than Fancy Pants. Now, I've thrown this pizza party because I've realized that I might not have been entirely honest the other day and I wanted to say sorry."

"You lied, Linda!" Sandra folded her arms.

"I did say you couldn't trust me. But look, pizza!" Linda thrust a slice of pepperoni pizza in Sandra's face.

Sandra held up a hand. "Pizza parties can't fix everything, Linda."

"They can't?" said Rex and Linda together.

"Look, I just want you all to like me! I might be the mayor, but I don't have any friends. I can be myself around you, even though you're sort of judgy."

Linda frowned at Sandra and Sandra frowned back.

"We need to know you've changed," Sandra said. "You can't go around pretending to be a human mayor and then use your powers to get people to do things for you that'll get them into trouble."

Rex thought about this. He had been thinking about disguises a lot and had a few new ideas. He leaned forward and started to talk to Linda.

"I think it's fine for you to use your mayor disguise if that makes you happy," Rex began.

"It does. I'm amazing as Jimmy Prigg," said Linda.

"I also think it would be fine to have an alien mayor not in disguise, like it's fine to have a dinosaur PE teacher and a dodo restaurateur."

"An alien mayor would be awesome!" added Sandra.

"But whatever you do," Rex continued, "I think you need to concentrate on things that help humans, like building parks and hospitals and holding a big festival of Cheez Nubbins called Nubbin Fest! I've got plans for that if you'd like some help…"

"Exactly!" said Sandra. "About doing good,

though Nubbin Fest sounds good too. Rex used his disguise skills to save the day for everyone on the spaceship. He's a hero and you could be the same."

"A hero!" Linda stood up and looked mistily into the distance. "I could be a hero and then the humans will love me even more! Jimmy Prigg: Hero Mayor! This I love."

"Great," said Sandra. "I think I'm ready for some pizza."

Linda slid her tentacles around the three of them again and pulled them in close.

"While you're here though, do you think you could do me a teensy-weensy favour?"

"Oh no..." groaned Sandra.

"Sure!" said Rex.

"When my agents reported to me about a dinosaur and a yeti living in the city, you weren't

the only undercover creatures they detected. There's something I'd like you to check out."

Linda pulled a fat file from under the sofa and dropped it on Rex's lap.

As Rex studied the file, he felt excitement shoot all the way from his tail to his eyebrows. If there were more creatures just like him in this city, he wanted to find them and help. He looked around the room at the others and smiled to himself. After all, even if you're in disguise, you still need friends.

FROM THE WINNER OF THE LAUGH OUT LOUD BOOK AWARDS

REX

DINOSAUR IN DISGUISE

ELYS DOLAN

BOOK 1 OUT NOW!

ABOUT THE AUTHOR

Elys Dolan makes books for children about everything from seagull detectives to weasels plotting world domination. She has won numerous awards, including the prestigious Lollies prize and the Alligator's Mouth Award for *Rex: Dinosaur in Disguise*. She is also a lecturer in Children's Book Illustration at the Cambridge School of Art.